HERBIE JONES

Moves On

HERBIE JONES

Moves On

By Suzy Kline

G. P. Putnam's Sons ★ New York

G. P. PUTNAM'S SONS,
a division of Penguin Putnam Books for Young Readers,
345 Hudson Street, New York, NY 10014.
G. P. Putnam's Sons, Reg. U.S. Pat. & Tm. Off.
Published simultaneously in Canada. Printed in the United States of America.
Book designed by Carolyn T. Fucile and Stefanie Rosenfeld.
Text set in New Caledonia.
Library of Congress Cataloging-in-Publication Data
Kline, Suzy. Herbie Jones moves on / by Suzy Kline.
p.   cm.   Summary: When his best friend's family plans
to move away, Herbie Jones does what he can to cope with the change.
[1. Moving, Household—Fiction. 2. Best friends—Fiction.
3. Friendship—Fiction. 4. Schools—Fiction.] I. Title.
PZ7.K6797 Hl 2003   [Fic]—dc21   2002032993
ISBN 0-399-23635-X
1   3   5   7   9   10   8   6   4   2
First Impression

Dedicated with love to my daughter
Jennifer Kline DeAngelis,
who always finds a way to move on.

Contents

Special thanks to my editor, Anne O'Connell,
for her questions and comments.
She was a valuable help in writing this manuscript.

Thanks to my husband, Rufus, for his thoughtful ideas.

Thanks to my friend Leah Kaplan, who told me
about a going-away party she once had for a student.
Her experience inspired this story.

And special appreciation to Robert McCloskey's *Homer Price*.

1

BAD NEWS

Herbie Jones was a fourth-grader.

He sat in the last row by the window next to the radiator. It was a rainy Monday in October, and his teacher, Miss Pinkham, was reading *Homer Price*. Everyone was listening to the story about the automatic donut maker.

Except for Raymond Martin. He was writing a note to Herbie. When he finished, he wadded it up into a tight ball and hit Herbie on the head with it.

"Ahhh!" Herbie jumped.

Annabelle Louisa Hodgekiss, who sat in front of him, turned around and said, "SHHHH!"

Herbie ignored her. He hated it when Annabelle acted like she ran the class. He unwrapped the ball of paper and read the note.

Dear Herb,
I have bad news. Its worse than loosing a dimund in a donut. I'm G O V M I N E
    Ray

Herbie looked over at Ray and wrinkled his eyebrows. "What's GOVMINE?" he whispered.

"Unscramble the word," Ray whispered back.

Herbie smiled. He and Ray liked using secret codes.

Herbie took out his small notepad from his back pocket and rewrote the letters *GOVMINE*.

Go me vin?

Mog evin?

Herbie continued to fiddle with the letters.

Mine vog?

Gone vim?

Vomeing?

Wait a minute! Herbie thought. He messed his

hair up so much thinking, it stuck out like porcupine quills.

MOVEING!

Ray couldn't spell it.

Herbie couldn't believe it.

"You're . . . MOVING?" Herbie whispered.

Ray nodded slowly three times.

No, no! Herbie thought. The news hit him like a block of ice.

Wham.

Herbie jerked back in his chair and barely caught himself from falling. As he clutched the desk, Miss Pinkham finished the story. ". . . *and the donuts kept right on rolling down the little chute just as regular as a clock can tick—they just kept right on a comin', an' a comin', an' a comin', an' a comin'.*"

Herbie closed his eyes and held back his tears. "Yeah," he mumbled. "And Ray is a goin', an' a goin', an' a goin', an' a goin'."

It *was* worse than losing a diamond in a donut. Herbie was losing his best friend.

2

SPAGHETTI AND TEXAS

Herbie and Ray sat at the end of the cafeteria table. As Ray gobbled down his spaghetti and garlic bread, Herbie barely touched his lunch. "How long have you known you were moving?" Herbie asked.

"Mom told me this morning," Ray replied, forking a meatball and popping it into his mouth.

Herbie pushed his plate away. "How can you eat at a time like this? We've been buddies forever. A *team*. We're baseball greats—Ray Mart and Herb Jones! How can that come to an end?"

Ray slurped his milk. "It won't. We'll still be

friends." Then he burped. "Are you gonna eat your gingerbread and whipped cream?" he asked.

"It's yours," Herbie groaned. "So, where are you moving to?"

"My dad has big plans to move to Texas."

"TEXAS?" Herbie exclaimed.

"What about Texas?" John Greenweed asked.

Now everyone at their lunch table had their eyes on Ray. Ray liked the attention. He decided to share his bad news with everyone. "I'm movin' to Texas."

Margie was the first to respond. "Oh, Ray. You can't go!"

"You lucky bum," Phillip said. "I bet you get to wear boots and cowboy hats, ride a horse, and have lots of barbecues."

John Greenweed offered Ray one of his mozzarella cheese sticks. "Will you send me a picture of an armadillo? That's my favorite animal. A lot live in Texas. They eat termites and scorpions."

Annabelle put the lid on her yogurt carton and cringed. Then she asked, "You're really going, Ray?" She seemed excited about the idea.

Ray leaned back in his chair as he finished his last bite of gingerbread. Some whipped cream was still on his upper lip. "Well, you know how it is. Here today, gone to . . ."

When Ray fell off his chair, everyone laughed. Except Herbie. He didn't think anything was funny. And Annabelle. She was annoyed. "When you fall like that, Ray, your chair scratches the floor," she complained.

"Will you guys miss me?" Ray asked as he got back up.

"Yeah." John Greenweed chuckled, noticing Ray's whipped cream mustache. "You make us laugh. Hey, we should give you a going-away party. When are you moving?"

Ray shrugged. "I don't know, but we're starting to pack things. It might be soon. Real soon."

Annabelle immediately crossed her fingers under the table. She was hoping it was true.

Herbie wiped his eyes with his shirtsleeve. He didn't want anyone to know his eyes were getting watery. "You need help packing?" he asked as his voice cracked.

"Yeah, everything's a mess at my house," Ray said. "Come over after school today."

Herbie nodded. He didn't say much the rest of the day.

3

*SHERIFF
HERBIE JONES*

When Herbie got home from school, his grandfather was watching a video. He was visiting their family for a few weeks again. As usual, he was enjoying a Western. Mr. and Mrs. Jones were at work. Herbie's sister, Olivia, had volleyball practice.

Hamburger Head left Grandpa Jones's feet and scooted over to meet Herbie. Herbie dropped to his knees, let his dog lick his face, then gave him a good hug and a back scratch. Herbie figured his granddad had given him a can of SpaghettiOs. The dog had tomato breath.

"Is that the movie *High Noon*?" Herbie asked.

The two of them had just watched it the night before.

"Yup. It seemed like a good way for Hamburger Head and me to spend a rainy afternoon. Want to watch it with me again?"

"No, thanks, Grandpa. I'm going over to Ray's house to help him pack."

"Is he going on a trip?"

"No. He's . . . moving." As soon as Herbie said it, he plopped down next to his granddad on the couch. "I don't want Ray to move."

Grandpa Jones put his arm around Herbie. After a long quiet moment, Herbie started to cry. He had kept it inside all day long. It was too hard now.

"I'll be lonely without him," he said.

"That's just how Sheriff Will Kane felt in *High Noon*. Remember? Only he felt like he didn't have *any* friends. He had to carry on alone."

"And he did, didn't he?" Herbie sat up and looked his granddad in the eye.

"He sure did. But he got some help from his wife."

Herbie made a face. He certainly wasn't getting married.

"Yeah," Grandpa continued, "Sheriff Will just moved on. You'll do that, too. You and Ray can write and keep in touch."

"Ray hates to write."

"You can visit him," Grandpa Jones suggested.

"In Texas?"

"Whoa . . . That *is* a long way from Connecticut," Grandpa Jones replied. "But you two are old friends. You'll figure out a way to keep in touch. *We* do. I'm from California, remember?"

Herbie stood up and nodded. "That's right, Grandpa!" Then he walked into the kitchen and grabbed an apple and two oatmeal cookies. He was feeling better about things. He always did after he talked with his granddad.

Five minutes later, Herbie put on his yellow rain slicker and headed over to Ray's house. For a few minutes he pretended he was Sheriff Will riding into town, facing the enemy. Herbie wished he had a badge. He also wished he knew who the enemy was.

When he turned down Wainwright Crescent, Herbie noticed the FOR SALE sign on Ray's front lawn. It swayed back and forth. As he got closer, he could hear it creak.

Ray's lawn was mowed. That's funny,' Herbie thought. Usually when he walked through Ray's grass, it was up to his knees. Shadow was sleeping on the front porch. Herbie stepped over the black shaggy dog and rang the doorbell.

Ray opened the door and slapped his buddy five. "Thanks for coming over," he said.

"No problem. Cookie?"

Ray popped it in his mouth. "Tasty. Olivia make it?"

"Yeah, she's been experimenting with all kinds of recipes in her cooking class. It's her favorite subject since Lance Pellizini joined her kitchen group."

Ray made a face. He didn't like hearing about any girl-boy stuff.

"Hi, Herbie!" Mrs. Martin said as she took Herbie's raincoat and hung it on a hook in the hall. Just as Herbie said hi, the phone rang.

"Oh, Ray!" she groaned. "You didn't put the phone back again. Help me find it, quick! It might be the Realtor."

The boys immediately started searching the messy living room for the cordless phone.

Herbie looked under some of the big boxes.

Mrs. Martin looked under the pillows.

After the fourth ring, Ray found it in the empty pizza box on the coffee table and handed it to his mom. There was a little tomato sauce on the mouthpiece.

The call was a short one.

"My goodness," Mrs. Martin said, returning the phone to its proper place on the wall. "The Realtor is bringing some people over in ten minutes! Who knows? Maybe they'll be the ones to buy our house!"

Herbie's eyeballs bulged.

Suddenly, he knew who the enemy was!

Now the question was, what was he going to do about it?

4

FOOLPROOF PLAN

"Time to wave the magic wand," Mrs. Martin joked. "Ray, go clean your room. Give it the ten-minute special. I'll do the ten-minute special down here." Then she ran for the vacuum cleaner.

Ray and Herbie trudged upstairs.

"We need a plan to outsmart the enemy," Herbie whispered.

Ray looked at his buddy. "Who's the enemy?"

"*Anyone* who wants to buy your house," Herbie snapped. "We have to outsmart them with one of our foolproof plans!"

Ray stepped into his room and plopped down

on his unmade bed. "I'm too tired to think," he whined, "and I don't feel like cleaning up."

Herbie clicked his fingers. "That's it!"

"What?" Ray groaned.

"Our foolproof plan."

Ray made a face. He didn't even ask to hear about it. "Remember our last enemy? The girls at that square dance? Well, our foolproof plan backfired. You ended up dancing with Annabelle and I got Margie. It was a real death sentence. I'm still not fully recovered."

Herbie laughed. "Well, this plan *is* foolproof. And you thought of it yourself, Ray. Just now!"

"I did?"

"You did," Herbie answered. "We just *don't* clean up. Those people will never want to buy this house after they see your room. It's a disaster."

Ray sat up and looked around at all the toys on the floor, the crumpled-up pieces of paper, and the smelly old socks. He grinned. "Yeah! And I just thought of something else I can do to make our plan a little more foolproof!"

At that very moment, lightning flashed through the window. Thunder rumbled and roared. And rain pelted the street, sidewalks, parked cars, and lawns.

But Herbie wasn't watching the storm outside. He was watching the one going on inside.

Storm Raymond!

5

STORM RAYMOND

Herbie watched Ray throw his pillows on the floor, dump a jar of fake spiders, and sprinkle the little red hotels from his Monopoly game onto the rug. When he emptied his Clue game, the wrench and lead pipe landed in the doorway. Professor Plum landed next to the silver horse that was rearing back on its heels.

"Yes!" Ray pumped his arm twice. "It's a regular minefield."

BZZZZZZZZZZZZZ! went the doorbell.

"The enemy!" Ray cackled. Then he dumped a bowl of dried-up oatmeal.

"That's gross!" Herbie said, staring at the brown glob on the rug.

"Our plan needed something else," Ray insisted.

Herbie nodded. He thought of something else it needed, too. He closed his eyes and said a silent prayer. *Please, Lord, keep Ray here. I don't want him to move away.*

"We just had a new roof put on," Mrs. Martin said when the people came inside the house.

Herbie and Ray scooted under the bed and hid.

"It's close to the school and shopping areas," the Realtor added. "And it has a nice backyard."

Mrs. Martin told the young couple why she wanted to move. "My husband has a job opportunity in Texas. And . . . we need a bigger home, too." After she patted her stomach, she added, "I'm five months pregnant."

Herbie bumped his head on the mattress springs. "Your mom is going to have a baby? Why didn't you tell me?"

Ray shrugged. "She told me two weeks ago. I was gonna tell you, but I forgot."

"You forgot?" Herbie elbowed Ray. "That's a

big part to forget. Just think, you'll have a sister or a brother. I hope you get a brother."

"Me, too," Ray replied. "I'm leaving if it's a girl."

Herbie laughed, then moved a smelly slipper away from his nose.

A few minutes later, the footsteps got louder. "Upstairs are the two bedrooms and a bathroom," the Realtor said.

Herbie and Ray rested their chins on their hands and listened, but didn't move an inch.

When the people entered the bedroom, Mrs. Martin squealed, "OOOOH, WHAT A MESS!"

Raymond didn't say boo.

"OOOOH! What did I step in?" the young lady squawked. She bent down and looked at the bottom of her shoe. "Aaaauuuugh! What is this brown, gooey stuff?"

Mrs. Martin rolled her eyes. "I am *so* sorry! It looks . . . like my son's breakfast."

"Ouch!" the young man squealed. He was wearing sandals and got the tiny silver horse piece caught between his toes.

The Realtor tried to keep things light. "Clue and Monopoly were my favorite games when I was a young boy!" he said, picking up a handful of game pieces.

The young couple didn't say a word.

"Why don't we look at the other bedroom," the Realtor suggested.

"Yes," Mrs. Martin agreed. "I'll talk with my son *later* about the condition of his room."

Ray shivered under the bed.

Herbie closed his eyes and said another quick prayer. *Lord, help Ray explain our foolproof plan to his mom. Make her understand we had to do it.*

When the people finally walked out the door, Ray and Herbie crawled out from under the bed and over to the window. They stayed on their knees as they peeked around the curtain. Mrs. Martin and the young couple were talking in the front yard under the Realtor's big black umbrella.

"It worked!" Ray said. "They're leaving!"

"I hope so," Herbie replied. "It's got a price, though, Ray. You'll be in hot water tonight. And I don't mean the kind you like in your bath."

"You haven't seen Part B yet, Herbie."

"Part . . . B?"

"We clean the room *now!* It will change Mom's mood from mad to glad."

Herbie stood up. "You know what, Ray? Part B just might do it."

When the boys finished cleaning up the room, they checked the window again. They didn't notice the people were still talking to the Realtor and Mrs. Martin behind their car.

But they noticed something else.

"Hey," Herbie said. "It stopped raining. You know what that means . . ."

"WORMS!" they both yelled. They dashed downstairs, grabbed their coats, and ran outside to the backyard.

6

THE PHONE CALL

The next morning before school, the phone rang. Olivia picked it up in the kitchen, after the first ring. She had her hair wrapped in a bath towel, and pimple cream on her face. "Hello?" she said in a soft, pleasing voice.

"Double 0 3 0?" Ray asked.

"ERB!" Olivia yelled. "IT'S FOR YOU." Herbie gulped his juice and then reached for the phone. He was glad they had finally gotten a cordless like Ray. Now he could talk in private under the table. "Hello?" he said in a muffled voice. "Yes, this is Double 0 3 0. How'd it go, 992?"

Olivia rolled her eyeballs as she made tuna

sandwiches with pickles and parsley for Herbie and herself. She thought their code names were dumb.

Ray got right to business. "Well, Herbie," he said, "Mom was pretty mad. She yelled at me right after you left. Then, after I walked her back up to my room and showed her what we did, she wasn't so mad. Just a little mad. But she said I couldn't go fishing with you Saturday morning."

"Why not?" Herbie asked. "We caught eighteen worms for bait! It won't cost anything."

"It's not about fish," Ray said. "It's about those two people yesterday . . ."

"Yeah . . ."

"They're buying the house."

"NOOOOOOOOOO!" Herbie screamed.

"Yeah. And it gets worse. I have to help Mom and Dad pack all weekend, and you can't help. Mom said we fool around too much. Talk to you later. On the corner."

Mr. Jones stuck his head out the bedroom door. "Can I get a little shut-eye around here?"

When the door slammed, Mrs. Jones said, "Kids, you know your dad works the swing shift now from three to eleven. It's better than the night shift he had, but he still needs to sleep longer than we do in the morning."

"It's not my fault," Olivia snapped, "that creeps like Raymond Martin call so early in the morning." Then she chopped the crusts off each sandwich briskly. *Chonk! Chonk! Chonk! Chonk!*

"He's not a creep!" Herbie snapped back. "HE'S MY FRIEND AND HE'S MOVING!"

Mrs. Jones put her coffee cup down. "Moving? The Martins are moving?"

"Ray's dad has a new job in Texas, and his mom is having a baby," Herbie blurted out.

Mrs. Jones raised her eyebrows. "Exciting, huh? Ray's mom stopped by and told me the other day when I was working at Dipping Donuts. She was surprised Ray hadn't told you yet. I said I'd wait until he did."

Mrs. Jones tousled her son's hair. "Well, whatever happens, I know you and Ray will continue to be friends."

"A baby," Olivia said in a dreamy voice.

"I hope Ray gets a brother," Herbie mumbled.

"THANKS, ERB!" That was the nickname

Olivia used when she was angry. It reminded her of smelly seasonings.

"YOU'RE WELCOME, OLIVE," Herbie replied. That was his favorite nickname for his sister. An olive was roly-poly and Olivia hated being called fat.

When Mr. Jones opened and slammed the door again, a small piece of plaster fell from the ceiling.

"I better go," Herbie said. "Bye, Mom. Bye, OLIVE." He put on his baseball cap, popped his lunch in his book bag, and stepped over the plaster. He was used to stuff like that happening ever since his dad had remodeled the kitchen himself.

"I love you, Herbie," his mom called. "Everything will work out for the best."

"I hope so," Herbie replied. "Maybe it'll take them a month to pack. There's a lot of stuff in Ray's house."

As Herbie stepped out the door, he waved to his granddad, who was walking Hamburger Head around the corner. Then he skipped down the stairs to meet Ray. There was still time for them to be together.

7

THE SECRET GIFT

That morning in class, Ray announced his big news. "Our house is sold. The people want to move in right away."

"Right away?" Herbie replied. "You didn't tell me that this morning."

"I forgot that part."

"You always forget the important parts," Herbie snapped.

"So you *are* moving?" Annabelle asked.

"DUH!" Herbie yelled in Annabelle's face. He was mad at everything and everyone.

Annabelle flared her nostrils. "Herbie Jones, I

like to double-check my facts. Unlike *some* people around here."

"I'm moving Sunday," Ray explained.

Miss Pinkham sighed. "Oh, Ray. Things aren't going to be the same without you."

"That means Friday is your last day in school," John Greenweed piped in. "We should have a going-away party that day."

"YEAH!" Everyone cheered.

Herbie slouched down in his chair. He didn't feel like having a party. You have a party when you are happy, he thought. Not when you are sad.

"Raymond," Miss Pinkham said, handing him a note. "Would you take this to Mrs. Read in the library for me?"

"Sure," Ray said.

Annabelle immediately shot up her hand. "*I'm* the messenger this week. *I* should take the note to the librarian."

Ray bolted. He always jumped at the chance to get out of class.

"I know," Miss Pinkham said softly. "I wanted Raymond to leave the room so we could talk about his going-away surprise. Maybe we could think of a little something to give him."

"Oh," Annabelle replied. "Well, my dad said if Ray moves, I *have* to give him a farewell gift."

"That's nice of your father," Miss Pinkham said. "But I'm talking about a class gift. From all of us. Anyone have a good idea?"

"Ray likes Viking ships," John said. "Maybe we could find a poster of one."

"Cool!" Phillip exclaimed. Then he picked his nose.

"Hey," Jose added. "Ray loves to eat. We should get him a cake."

"Good idea, Jose. I'll order one from Price Busters," Miss Pinkham said.

Margie raised her hand. "We could give Ray a T-shirt and then we could all sign our names on it with a purple pen. Purple is his favorite color."

Annabelle objected. "I think we should use different colors."

"I have plenty of Magic Markers," Miss Pinkham said. "We could use the permanent ones I keep in my bottom drawer."

"Let's vote!" John said. "Ray'll be coming back any minute."

"You're right," Miss Pinkham agreed. "All in favor of the Viking poster?"

John and Phillip were the only ones who raised their hands.

"The T-shirt idea?"

Everyone else raised their hands.

"It's settled, then. I'll pick up a T-shirt after school today," Miss Pinkham said.

Margie clapped her hands. "It's going to be a great party!"

Great? Herbie thought. I don't think so. This was one party he wished would never happen.

8

HANGING OUT

That afternoon, Ray went over to Herbie's house after school. Ray's parents had a meeting at the real estate office. The sun was out and so was Grandpa Jones, raking the front lawn. "Hi, boys! What do you think of all these leaves?" he asked.

Herbie dropped his book bag on the ground and sat next to his dog. He didn't feel like talking.

"Yeah, the trees are losin' lots of leaves," Ray answered as he plopped down on the grass. "Pretty soon everything will be different."

Herbie nodded.

"So," Grandpa Jones said, "you two have homework tonight?"

"Just a minute talk on any topic," Herbie said, removing a flea from Hamburger Head's ear.

Ray knew his topic already. "I'm talking about leaving."

Grandpa Jones nodded. "Speaking of *leave*-ing … look at these specimens."

Herbie looked up. His grandfather had a handful of leaves.

"You've got three kinds on your lawn, Herbie. This colorful one here is maple. But this fan-shaped leaf is a ginkgo. The ginkgo tree was around during the age of the dinosaurs. Some things just last and last. Like your friendship."

When Herbie passed the tiny leaf to Raymond, he tried to fan himself with it.

Grandpa Jones continued, "And this leaf here that looks like a mitten is a sassafras."

Herbie went over to the big maple tree and climbed out to a branch. When he dropped to his knees, he was hanging upside down. "Hey, Ray," he said, "your mouth looks like one big eyeball."

Ray joined him up in the tree. As he was hanging the same way, he called down to Herbie's granddad, "You must be from the same galaxy, your mouth looks like one big eyeball, too."

Grandpa Jones chuckled. "Hang around, guys, and I'll take you for a spin in my spaceship."

"Hey, Ray," Herbie said. "Wanna take a spin in our *own* spaceship?"

"MAN THE CONTROLS, DOUBLE 0 3 0!" Ray yelled. "LET'S BLAST OFF!"

Grandpa Jones waved as he headed to the house. "See you guys later. I'm blasting off myself for some coffee."

"Over and out!" the boys yelled.

"And now . . . to a new galaxy!" Herbie called.

"Neeeeooow! Neeeeooow!" Herbie and Ray waved their hands madly in the air.

Just as their rocket ship was going full blast, Annabelle Louisa Hodgekiss showed up on Herbie's front lawn. "Hi, boys!" she said. "I'm on my way home from Margie's house. We were practicing our speeches for tomorrow. You two playing rocket ship?"

Herbie and Ray exchanged a look.

"Annabelle!" Ray groaned. "Quick! Time to self-destruct!"

Both boys fell limp.

When Annabelle walked over to the tree, she looked up at the hanging boys. They were perfectly still. Like sleeping bats.

Annabelle laughed. "Eh . . . Ray, did Herbie tell you I'm giving you a farewell gift?"

Ray immediately opened his eyes wide and sat up on the branch. "No, he didn't. What is it?"

Herbie gritted his teeth. The last thing he wanted to do was hang out with Annabelle.

But she shimmied up the tree and joined them anyway. "It's neat up here," she said. "Kind of reminds me of the balance beam. Hey, can you guys do this?"

Boy, Herbie thought. She's been here forty seconds, and already she's showing off.

Herbie and Ray watched Annabelle drop to her knees, and then to her ankles. As she hung from the branch, she swung her hands back and forth. They almost touched the ground.

"I'm taking gymnastics now," Annabelle explained. "There are certain techniques you have to know, like dismounting. Watch." She dropped to the ground and rolled into a double somersault. Then she jumped to her feet, stood tall with her hands in the air, and said, "Tah-dah! Want to try?"

"Piece of cake," Ray answered. "Let's do it, Herb!"

The boys dropped down to their knees just fine. They had been doing that all afternoon. But when they tried to drop farther, to their ankles, they both slipped and tumbled to the grass.

"Ouch! Oooooh!" the boys said.

Annabelle giggled. "Well, you haven't had the practice time I've had. You should go to gymnastics instead of playing rocket ship."

Herbie glared at Annabelle. And *you* should go to Texas! he thought.

"See you, boys!" Then she petted Hamburger Head a few times and left.

Ray stuffed three blades of grass in his mouth. "Darn, I didn't find out what Annabelle is giving me for a going-away gift."

Herbie snarled, "Want to find out what *I'm* giving you?"

"Sure!" Ray replied.

"This!" Herbie jumped on Raymond. He pinned his shoulders to the ground with his knees and tickled him good under the arms.

"HELP! GRANDPA JONES, SAVE ME!"

9

BUZZ!

Wednesday afternoon, Miss Pinkham moved a desk in front of the class, then set a box on top that had PODIUM printed on it in big red letters.

"It's time to begin our one-minute talks," she announced. "The topic was your choice. Anything from Abe Lincoln to fried eggs. Volunteers?"

Annabelle Louisa Hodgekiss raised her hand immediately and went first. Herbie knew she would. Annabelle always had to be first.

"I'll let Raymond do the buzzer," Miss Pinkham said.

A lot of people nodded. It was the fair thing to do. This was Raymond's last week.

Ray grinned. He loved being "it." He took the little blue buzzer that was once part of a board game and buzzed it once. *Bzzzzzz!* "It works!" he said.

Miss Pinkham smiled.

As soon as the red second hand left the twelve, Annabelle began. "My topic is Amelia Earhart. Many of you know this brave woman died a heroine somewhere in the Pacific Ocean. She was the first *woman* to fly across the Atlantic Ocean in 1932. She was the first *person* to fly between California and Hawaii in 1935. She did it before any man did it."

John Greenweed and Phillip McDoogle made a face.

Bzzzz! Ray accidentally buzzed the buzzer too soon. "Sorry, you have thirty seconds left."

Annabelle flared her nostrils and then continued. "Amelia Earhart carried chicken soup on her flights, and hot cocoa. When she got off the plane, she didn't like people to come near her. I know why. I listened to a special documentary on her on TV and found out the reason. It was because—"

Bzzzz! Ray buzzed the buzzer. "TIME'S UP!"

Annabelle looked at the teacher.

Miss Pinkham was annoyed with Ray and her tone of voice showed it. "*Please* continue, Annabelle. You left us with a real cliff-hanger. Why didn't Amelia Earhart like crowds to come too close?"

Annabelle lowered her voice. "Because she wasn't able to go to the bathroom during her long flights, she had lots of accidents."

"You mean she crashed?" Ray blurted out.

"No." John sneered. "Annabelle's talking about bathroom accidents. In those days, you didn't leave the cockpit for *anything.*"

Ray couldn't believe it. His face turned very serious. "Not even for number two?"

"No," Annabelle continued in an adult manner. "So . . . Amelia Earhart would usually have an offensive aroma when she got off the plane, and would hurry over to the hangar. After she changed into fresh clothes, she would talk to people."

As soon as Annabelle finished her speech, Miss Pinkham started clapping.

"Excellent job," the teacher said. "You talked about a sensitive matter, and a very practical one, too."

Raymond buzzed the buzzer twice. *Bzzzz! Bzzzz!* "I agree!" he said. "When you gotta go, you gotta go!"

Annabelle shot Ray a look as she returned to her seat.

After most of the kids spoke at the podium, including Herbie, who talked about the three kinds of leaves on his front lawn, Raymond went up.

"You can choose someone to do the buzzer for your talk," the teacher said.

Everyone looked at Herbie. Ray always picked Herbie. Ray started toward Herbie but then turned and handed it to Annabelle.

Annabelle sat up straight and beamed. She was thrilled. Herbie wrinkled his eyebrows. Why didn't Ray pick me? he wondered. And this was his last week he'd be picking people, too!

Annabelle gently rested her hand on the blue buzzer. She was very careful not to touch it before it was time.

Raymond began his speech. "You all know I'm moving and that Friday is my last day in this classroom. Most of our stuff is in boxes now, and our phone is even disconnected.

"My dad has a friend in Texas who has a big job for him. That's why we're moving.

"As soon as I get there, I'll send John a picture of an armadillo and take pictures of my first barbecue. I plan on taking horseback-riding lessons. Maybe for my next birthday, I'll get a horse."

Herbie rolled his eyeballs.

Ray continued, "And I plan on visiting the Alamo. I want to see Jim Bowie's knife and Davy Crockett's raccoon hat. It's nice you guys are giving me a farewell party on—"

Bzzzzzzz! Annabelle buzzed the buzzer.

"Friday," Ray finished, and then he sat down.

While everyone clapped, Herbie groaned. "Thanks for picking *me*."

Ray grinned. "Hey, Annabelle is giving me a special present. I figured if I called on her, she might get me a real good one. I'll share it with you, whatever it is."

Herbie rapped his pencil on the desk. Raymond could act so dumb sometimes. Why should he care if he was leaving?

"Oh why don't *you* go fly a plane," Herbie snarled.

Ray looked at his buddy.

Herbie wasn't smiling.

He wasn't joking.

He was angry.

Ray put his head down on his desk. Things weren't turning out the way he wanted. Now his best friend was mad at him.

10

GETTING READY

Friday, October 19, was a day Herbie never wanted to come.

But it did.

That afternoon at 1:30 P.M., Miss Pinkham sent Ray out of the room again.

Ray didn't object. He and Herbie weren't getting along that great. Nothing was fun anymore.

"The librarian told me she had a surprise for you," Miss Pinkham added.

Ray nodded. "I know. She told me. She's giving me *The History of Hamburgers* for a going-away present since it's my . . . last day here."

Ray didn't realize he was going to choke on the last three words.

As soon as he left, everyone started making cards for him. At 1:45 several people finished.

"Can we write on the blackboard?" Margie asked.

Miss Pinkham looked at the clock. She knew she wasn't going to squeeze in much more that day. The party was *it*. "What a good idea, Margie. Go ahead. Anyone else can, too."

Annabelle and Sarah Sitwellington joined Margie and wrote good-luck messages to Ray on the board. Afterward, they passed out Baggies of gumdrops, and arranged brightly colored yellow and purple mums on the cake table. Annabelle folded the flowery napkins she brought in the shape of diamonds.

Phillip and John dumped tortilla chips in one bowl, and salsa in another.

Miss Pinkham took the sheet cake out of the box. It said BON VOYAGE, RAYMOND! in purple frosting. And there was a ship on it. Ray had written that once on a get-well card to Annabelle. The teacher knew it was his favorite greeting.

Jose collected all the farewell cards and put them in a special yellow folder he had made. He wrote, HAVE FUN WITH THE ARMADILLOS! on the outside.

At 1:55 P.M., while John and Phillip helped the teacher pass out the fruit punch, Herbie was still writing. He never could stay mad at Ray for very long. He wanted his card to be really special. After all, Ray was his best friend.

At 2:00 P.M., Miss Pinkham walked over to the intercom. "I'll call Mrs. Read now and tell her to send Ray back to the room."

"Hey, let's hide!" John Greenweed suggested. "Maybe he'll think we went somewhere, and then when he walks in the classroom, we can jump up and yell 'SURPRISE!'"

Everyone agreed that was a good idea and hid under their desks. Even the teacher.

No one moved.

The first minute, the class was pin quiet.

The second minute, people started whispering.

The third minute, people started shushing other people.

The fourth minute, Miss Pinkham stood up and

went over to the intercom. "Mrs. Read?" she called.

"Yes?"

"Did Raymond Martin leave the library?"

"He sure did. About two minutes ago."

"Thank you."

"EVERYONE DOWN!" John yelled.

After a long minute passed, Phillip whispered, "I hear footsteps! Ray's coming!"

Everyone ducked under their desks again.

And waited.

11

WHERE'S RAY?

The person who stepped into the classroom got a big "SURPRISE!"

"Oh, dear!" Mrs. Read said. "I'm sorry, kids. It's just me." The librarian had three pencils stuck in the bun in the back of her head. Each had an eraser on top in the shape of a ship. The ships looked like the ones Columbus sailed in.

The children popped up from under their desks and groaned. "Where's Ray?"

"Maybe he's washing his hands," Mrs. Read suggested. "He had Magic Marker all over them! He'll be here any minute. I just stopped by to bring the picture he made for you. He left it in the library."

Everyone looked at Ray's drawing of a Viking ship. Ray had drawn twenty-one Vikings on board.

"That's us!" John replied. "There's twenty-one in our class. The lady in the crow's nest with blond hair must be Miss Pinkham."

"What a treasure!" the teacher exclaimed.

Miss Pinkham took the drawing and taped it to the blackboard.

Mrs. Read looked around the room at all the decorations and food. "Everything looks great, boys and girls. Back to your stations!"

Everyone hid again behind their desks.

Except Miss Pinkham.

She walked the librarian to the doorway and whispered, "Please check the hallways for Raymond. I'm getting worried."

Herbie turned and looked outside the window.

There was a dark cloud in the sky. It looked just like the shape of Texas.

Where in the world was Ray?

12

THE FOOD SIDE

Raymond was sitting outside the kindergarten room, bawling.

Like a kindergarten baby, he thought.

He was glad the classroom door was closed.

When Mrs. Read found him, he quickly wiped his eyes with his sleeve. He didn't like anyone else seeing him cry. The librarian sat down next to him on the new green carpet.

"I've been wandering the halls looking for you, Raymond. Your classmates and teacher are waiting for you. What's wrong?"

"Everything." Ray sniffled.

"Like what?" Mrs. Read asked.

"Like leaving Herbie and all my friends. It just hit me when I was walking back from the library. I felt like I was walking to the electric chair. My life here is over."

The librarian smiled, then put her arm around Ray. "I know, it's hard. Leaving is never easy."

Ray's voice trembled. "I thought if I didn't go to the surprise party, maybe it might not happen. So I came here. Where it's safe."

"Oh, Ray," Mrs. Read said, patting his shoulder. "You're so friendly, you're going to make lots of new friends in Texas. And you'll keep all your old friends, like Herbie. Let's go back to your room now and enjoy the party everyone's planned for you."

Ray stopped crying. But he didn't move. He just stayed slouched down against the wall.

"You know, Ray . . . it helps to look on the good side of things like . . ." Mrs. Read pointed to the colorful family pictures that the kindergartners had painted. They were displayed on the wall across from them.

"Like you'll still be with your mom and dad,

your dog, and you're going to have a new brother or sister. They're all going with you to Texas."

"Yeah, it better be a brother," Ray snapped. But he didn't budge.

Mrs. Read chuckled. When she noticed the hamburger book on his lap, she added, "And, of course, it helps to look on the food side, too."

"The food side?" Ray sat up.

"Yes," she explained, "the cake, the gumdrops, the punch, the tortilla chips and salsa, and the Rice Krispie squares are waiting for you. . . ."

Ray stood up and hummed, "Mmm . . . food. I forgot that part." His sad mood seemed to be lifting.

"Ready to go to your party now?" Mrs. Read asked.

"I'm ready," Ray said. He took off like a rocket for the classroom. "Neeeeooow! Neeeeooow!"

13

*URPRI*E!

"RAY'S COMING!" Phillip screamed from under his desk.

"Shhhh!" Annabelle scolded.

As soon as Ray walked through the doorway, everyone jumped up and yelled, "SURPRISE!"

Herbie rushed over to Ray. "You're here! Man, where have you been? I was worried about you."

"You were?" Ray asked. "You're not mad any-more about my picking Annabelle instead of you?"

"Nah, it's history," Herbie said.

Just as he and Ray slapped each other five, all the kids gathered around. Mrs. Read and Miss Pinkham did, too.

"Sorry to keep you guys waiting," Ray apologized. "I was . . . checking out the new carpet outside the kindergarten room. It's nice. No fuzz balls." He and Mrs. Read exchanged smiles.

Miss Pinkham didn't appreciate his humor. "Next time you take a detour, Raymond Martin, remember to ask permission first. A teacher needs to know where a student is at *all times.* It's an important rule."

"Sorry," Ray repeated. "I won't do it in Texas." Then he waved to Mrs. Read as she headed for the door.

"Okay, you guys, enough of this babbling! It's time to party!" John ordered.

"YEAH, PARTY!" Phillip yelled.

Jose reached for his folder of greetings and handed them to Ray.

"Gee, these are all for me?" Ray asked.

"Yes!" Margie said. "Now you get to sit in the Author's Chair and wear this crown. I got it special from Burger Paradise."

Ray beamed as Margie put the hat on his head and sang out, "King Raymond!"

Then she picked out Herbie's card for him to read first.

"Cool hammerhead shark," Ray said, looking at the picture Herbie had drawn of them fishing together.

"We catch the big ones," Herbie replied. Then he handed Ray one of his Rice Krispie bars.

"Mmmm, thanks!" Ray said, biting into the crispy treat. When Ray glanced at the two verses of poetry, he asked Herbie to read his card aloud. There was an S word, and a C word that he didn't recognize.

Ray also wanted to concentrate on eating.

Herbie began reading:

Ray, Ray
Moving away
Moving to Texas any day
I wish he could
Be here with me
Sitting in a sassafras tree.

Herbie turned the page and read the second verse:

Ray, Ray
Why can't you stay?
We could fish and swim
And laugh and play.
You better write
And visit often
But if you don't pick me next time,
You'll be in a coffin.

    Your buddy,
    Herb Jones

After everybody laughed, Ray opened up the rest of the cards. When he came to Annabelle's, he looked for a present. Where was it? He looked on the floor and under the chair, but there was no gift.

"It's inside the card," Annabelle said.

Ray grinned as he ripped open the envelope. Inside was a homemade card folded into thirds. One picture was drawn neatly in each of the three spaces.

"Nice bird, flower, and bowling ball," Ray said politely.

Annabelle flared her nostrils. "I drew the state symbols of Texas, Raymond Martin. The first is a mockingbird, the second is a bluebonnet, and that bowling ball is a *pecan* from the state tree of Texas."

"Oh." Ray was more interested in the gift. He quickly looked inside the envelope again. When he pulled out a coupon book, he cheered, "Yahoo! Five one-dollar coupons to Burger Paradise! Thanks!"

"Don't thank me, thank my dad," Annabelle corrected. "It was his idea. He knows you love cheeseburgers. Remember when you and Herbie sneaked off during our field trip to get one?"

"Yup." Ray grinned.

"Yeah." Herbie smiled.

"Yes," Miss Pinkham said, rolling her eyeballs.

After all the cards were opened, Margie brought the class gift to Ray. It was wrapped in purple paper with a purple bow. "We are going to miss you very, very, very much," she said.

Ray ripped open the class gift in three seconds. When he held up the yellow T-shirt, he grinned from ear to ear. He loved the pictures and words, and everyone's signature. He pointed right away to the bloody vampire, Charlotte the spider, and the cheeseburger.

When Ray put it on over his school clothes, the T-shirt touched his knees. "Man, I like this! Thanks, guys!"

Herbie took out a small camera and snapped a picture of Ray in his special autographed shirt.

"My turn," Margie said, taking Herbie's camera.

"Let me take one of you and Ray. Your last day of school together!"

When Herbie and Ray stood side by side, Miss Pinkham looked like she was going to cry. "Don't forget to write us, Ray," she said.

After Margie snapped the picture, Ray went over and hugged his teacher good-bye. "I won't forget you," Ray said, wiping his eyes.

Everyone else lined up to give Raymond a hug. Even Annabelle.

Although she was at the end of the line.

"I didn't think I'd feel sad, but I do now," Annabelle confessed. Then she covered her face.

As soon as the Annabelle hug was over, Ray whispered to Herbie, "Am I still alive?"

Herbie rolled his eyes. "Not if Annabelle heard you ask that."

BRRRRRRRRRRING! went the dismissal bell.

Everyone gathered their things and lined up to go home. Miss Pinkham led the class out while a chorus of *GOOD-BYE, RAYMOND!*s echoed through the hall.

When the boys got outside, Herbie and Ray didn't say anything. They just kicked a rock along the sidewalk, taking turns to keep it on track.

When they got to the corner, Ray started to say the *G* word. "Well, since we're going to be busy loading the van this weekend, I guess this is *good-bye.*"

"Yeah," Herbie groaned. He couldn't look at Raymond. It was too hard.

Just when the boys were at their gloomiest, Ray remembered something. "Hey! We can't forget the food side!" he exclaimed, and he reached for the coupon book in his pocket. "We can say good-bye at Burger Paradise! Split a large order of Bits

O'Chicken, fries, and a shake! And it's all on Annabelle!"

"All right!" Herbie said as the boys leaped in the air, slapped each other ten with both hands, then bolted to Burger Paradise.

Together for the last time . . .

14

MONDAY BLUES

Monday morning, Herbie didn't feel like eating. Olivia had made him some cinnamon pinwheels, but he didn't even try one.

"It will take a while," Mrs. Jones said. "You and Ray did so much together."

"You know, Herbie, you can have more than one best friend," Olivia said gently. "Ray in Texas, and one here. I have three best friends. It's easier."

Somehow Olivia's words of wisdom didn't help. Herbie pushed his orange juice away. He didn't feel like drinking, either.

"Do you want me to drive you to school, dear?" Mrs. Jones offered.

Herbie looked over at his granddad. He was dunking a cinnamon pinwheel in his coffee. "Nah, I'll walk. I've gotta . . . move on."

"Just like that Sheriff Will did," Grandpa Jones piped up. "I'm proud of you, Herbie."

"Here's your lunch," Olivia said. "I packed some oatmeal raisin cookies and your favorite sandwich, peanut butter and jelly. I left the crusts on this time, the way you like it."

Olivia always mothered Herbie when he was sad about something.

"Thanks, Olive . . . ," Herbie muttered.

When Hamburger Head followed him to the door, Herbie turned, kneeled down, and gave him an extra-long hug. "At least I have you," he sighed.

Herbie could feel his dog's rapid heartbeat and his warm fur next to him. His tail beat the floor like a drumroll. "Wish me luck," Herbie said, getting up.

Hamburger Head barked twice.

When Herbie got to the corner, he lingered for a few minutes. Maybe Ray would appear if he yelled his name. "RAYMOND!" Herbie shouted.

Everything was so quiet. Even the yellow, orange, and brown leaves that zigzagged to the ground didn't make a noise.

Raymond Martin wasn't coming.

He was gone for good.

It was time for Herbie to move on by himself like Sheriff Will in *High Noon*.

Herbie tried to walk across the street, but he couldn't pick up his feet. They were stuck to the pavement like two bricks in cement. He said a silent prayer. *Lord, I need your help, real bad!*

Then he waited. And waited.

"Hey, Herbie. Want to walk with us?"

Herbie looked up. It was Margie calling from across the street. Annabelle was with her.

The idea wasn't a bad one. Even Sheriff Will got some help from his wife. At least he didn't have to marry Margie or Annabelle. "Might as well," Herbie mumbled.

Herbie didn't mind listening to Annabelle's update about Amelia Earhart. There was a rumor that she never did crash in the Pacific and die. She was alive and well as a grandmother in New Jersey.

"Someday," Annabelle added, "they're going to find her plane at the bottom of the ocean."

And someday, Herbie thought, I'll go to Texas to see Ray.

When they got to class, Herbie sat down, took out his notebook, and started drawing fish. He didn't want to look at Raymond's empty desk.

At 9:04 A.M., Miss Pinkham started another episode in *Homer Price.* It was about a skunk and a robbery. Herbie Jones put his pencil down and listened.

At 9:09 A.M., the teacher stopped reading right in the middle of a sentence.

Someone walked into the room.

RAYMOND MARTIN!

Everyone stared at him like he was a ghost. Herbie did a double take. Is this a mirage? he wondered.

"Ray . . . Raymond?" Miss Pinkham stuttered. "Did . . . you forget s-something?"

Mrs. Martin stepped into the room and explained things. "That job in Texas fell through. It's kind of a long story. We turned down the offer on the house, and . . . we're staying. We've decided just to add on a room to our old house."

Herbie threw his hands in the air. Yahoo! he thought. Then he bowed his head for a quick prayer. *Thank you, Lord!*

Ray grinned. "Did you guys miss me?"

Annabelle folded her arms as she looked up at the wall clock. "Raymond, you've been absent a total of fourteen minutes." Then she lowered her voice. "I can't believe I actually hugged you good-bye! May I have the book of coupons back, please?"

"Can't do that." Ray grinned. "Herbie and I already ate 'em."

Annabelle flared her nostrils as Herbie jumped out of his chair and gave his buddy a hug!

Miss Pinkham went over to talk privately with Mrs. Martin.

"I'm so sorry," Mrs. Martin whispered to the teacher. "I'm embarrassed about all the fanfare Ray got and here we are again."

Miss Pinkham shook her head. "Don't be. These things happen. I'm happy we get to keep Ray."

John made a face. "No armadillos."

As soon as Mrs. Martin left, Ray returned to his seat, and Miss Pinkham returned to her chair. When Ray realized his classmates were still looking at him, he said, "Hey, you guys wanna give me a welcome-back party?"

No one said anything.

They just kept staring at Raymond in disbelief.

Miss Pinkham stared, too.

The only one who smiled was Herbie. "Yeah," he said. "Now it *is* time to party!"